AN AUDIENCE CALLED ÉDOUARD

Also by David Pownall

Novels
AFRICAN HORSE
THE RAINING TREE WAR
GOD PERKINS
MY ORGANIC UNCLE *and other stories*
LIGHT ON A HONEYCOMB

Plays
MUSIC TO MURDER BY
THE DREAM OF CHIEF CRAZY HORSE

Poetry
ANOTHER COUNTRY
(*Peterloo*)

AN AUDIENCE CALLED ÉDOUARD

DAVID POWNALL

FABER AND FABER
London & Boston

*First published in 1979
by Faber and Faber Limited
3 Queen Square London WC1N 3AU
Printed in Great Britain by
Latimer Trend & Company Ltd Plymouth
All rights reserved*

© *1979 by David Pownall*

All rights whatsoever in this play are strictly
reserved and applications to perform it, etc. must
be made in advance, before rehearsals begin, to
John Johnson, Clerkenwell House,
45–47 Clerkenwell Green, London EC1

CONDITIONS OF SALE
*This book is sold subject to the condition that it shall not, by way
of trade or otherwise, be lent, re-sold, hired out or otherwise
circulated without the publisher's prior consent in any form of
binding or cover other than that in which it is published and
without a similar condition including this condition being
imposed on the subsequent purchaser*

British Library Cataloguing in Publication Data

Pownall, David
An Audience called Édouard.
I. Title
822'.9'14   PR6066. 9995A/

ISBN 0-571-11411-3

For Andrew Hewson in friendship

Characters

VICTORINE	25
BERTHE	28
FERDINAND	25
GUSTAVE	25
HUGO	45
ÉRIQUE	25

October 1862. France

The first performance of *An Audience Called Édouard* was given at the Greenwich Theatre on 19th October 1978. The cast was as follows:

FERDINAND	David Robb
VICTORINE	Susan Hampshire
GUSTAVE	Jeremy Irons
BERTHE	Stephanie Beacham
HUGO	David Burke
ÉRIQUE	James Taylor

The production was directed by Alan Strachan

ACT ONE

A glade with small conifers, yew and holly on an island in the Seine. One shore, and the opposite bank of the river at Argenteuil, are seen as background.

A rowing-boat is drawn up under the trees up-stage left, its oars parked across the well of the craft.

A young woman of Junoesque build, her dark hair up in a classical style, is paddling. She is dressed in a white, semi-transparent, roomy shift which has slid off her right (down-stage) shoulder as she dips her hand in the water. This is BERTHE.

Front-stage right is a heap of discarded clothes—a long blue dress, a straw bonnet with a black band and blue bow, a shift—and an overturned wicker basket from which apples, plums, green melons and cherries have tumbled on to the grass. A small, knobbly golden loaf lies beside the fruit. There has been a picnic.

Front-stage centre three fungi are growing.

Centre-stage sits VICTORINE, *naked. She has a young, well-fleshed, ivory-hued body. Her chestnut hair is drawn back from her face and braided in a thick ring round her head. She looks at the audience with a bold, collected stare: her right elbow resting on her raised right knee, her right hand cupping her chin. Her left leg lies bent and flat against the grass, the sole of her foot flat on to the audience. She is sitting on a light blue cloak which is also wrapped round her left (up-stage) leg.*

Close to her, slighty up-stage and to the up-stage left, sits GUSTAVE, *a young man in a brown frock-coat, cream trousers, shirt and tie. He has a short brown beard and a moustache.* GUSTAVE *is looking to the left of* VICTORINE's *gaze, his expression sad and thoughtful.*

FERDINAND *reclines to the left of* GUSTAVE *and* VICTORINE, *his legs spread to either side of* VICTORINE's *bare right foot. He is wearing a dark green frock-coat and light grey trousers, a light pink cravat and a round peakless cap with a hanging tassle. In his left hand (downstage) he holds a short cane with a hooked handle, his elbow (left) propped upon a bank beneath a prominent tree.* FERDINAND *has a full black beard and moustache and is facing* VICTORINE, *his right hand raised towards her as if illustrating a conversational point with a gesture.*

The characters remain perfectly still in these positions for ten seconds.

FERDINAND: (*Completing the gesture*) And where will the Suez Canal get us?
VICTORINE: Suez.
GUSTAVE: That's where you're wrong.
FERDINAND: It means France is getting deeper and deeper into debt.
GUSTAVE: The Egyptians have stopped working on it. The whole thing has come to a dead stop right in the middle of the desert. They'll never finish it.
BERTHE: The government says they will. . . .
FERDINAND: The *Emperor* says they will. Let's be precise about who is saying what. It's the Emperor who supports the canal. . . .
VICTORINE: But what use is it?
BERTHE: To get the navy out to Vietnam in double-quick time.
GUSTAVE: The Egyptians don't trust the French. That's why they've downed tools.
VICTORINE: Well, it's not their canal is it?
FERDINAND: It will be in ninety-nine years' time. We've promised them that.
VICTORINE: The men digging it aren't bothered about that. Do you work for your great-grandchildren or yourself?
FERDINAND: A bit of both.
GUSTAVE: It's stuck at Ismailia. Can you imagine what it must be like out there now? All the supervisors are going mad . . . I don't want to think about it. (*Pause*) Why do we have a navy

anyway? So Édouard can paint it, of course.
BERTHE: I'd like a break now, Édouard. It's getting chilly in here. . . .
FERDINAND: Give him a little while longer. He's working well today.
BERTHE: Swop places then. My back is breaking.
GUSTAVE: Édouard disliked the navy. He found the sea and sky tedious all the way to Rio de Janeiro. But not the carnival, eh, Édouard? What a young devil he was. . . .
BERTHE: (*Moving*) I'm getting out. Too late if you haven't got all you want. You must work faster.
FERDINAND: Give him another minute. . . .
BERTHE: Sorry, I'm getting out.
(BERTHE *gets out of the water*.)
VICTORINE: We're moving, Édouard.
BERTHE: You must have most of what you want by now.
FERDINAND: Hold on, let's see. Do you mind if we break the pose Édouard? We can go on if you want us to.
BERTHE: Oh no we can't. The bottom half of my legs have turned blue.
VICTORINE: (*Wrapping herself in the blue cloak she is sitting on*) October's getting a bit late for this lark.
FERDINAND: Come on, it's warm.
VICTORINE: You're warm, Ferdy.
BERTHE: Are you sitting on the towel, Victorine? Don't get up, I can get it. (*She pulls a towel from under* VICTORINE, *who edges off it*.) I don't like the feel of that mud. It's slimy and I keep expecting worms and things crawling over my toes. . . .
FERDINAND: You find crocodiles in the Seine you know.
GUSTAVE: They're in the Nile, and the Suez Canal, thousands of crocodiles, waiting. They've eaten half the labour force.
VICTORINE: Will you open that wine, Ferdy? I need something to warm me up inside.
BERTHE: Me too. Mind if I get close, Victorine? I'm frozen.
(BERTHE *dries her legs and leans back against* VICTORINE, *rubbing against her*.)
VICTORINE: Come and have some wine, Édouard. Wash the taste of paint away.

GUSTAVE: Victorine, I have just been thinking—do you know what your best feature is?

VICTORINE: What d'you mean? The one that looks best or the one that works best?

FERDINAND: A good distinction from one who knows.

GUSTAVE: Both.

VICTORINE: Both?

GUSTAVE: Yes, both.

(*Pause*)

VICTORINE: Gustave, you have not got much imagination.

GUSTAVE: It's your ears.

VICTORINE: Well, thank you, Gustave.

GUSTAVE: They're superb.

VICTORINE: I don't think so.

GUSTAVE: Ferdy, I appeal to you.

FERDINAND: No, I agree with Victorine. Her ears are a little large for my taste.

GUSTAVE: I'm not asking you to eat them.

VICTORINE: They are too big. They used to call me 'Elephant Ears' at school.

GUSTAVE: Édouard loves your ears. (*Pause*) He always insists that you show them. See, today ... every time he uses you, it's the ears he's after. Victorine, I am in desperate need of your ears.

BERTHE: What about the rest of her?

GUSTAVE: Not indifferent but ... I don't feel the same way about that. Just those beautiful, luscious, classical ears.

VICTORINE: Gustave, if you'll give me a regular allowance, an apartment, a bank account ... you can have an affair with my ears.

FERDINAND: One at a time or simultaneously?

VICTORINE: We'll have to work that out.

BERTHE: I wouldn't trust Gustave to behave like a gentleman. Don't sell anything to him, not even your ears. Keep your ears pure, love.

GUSTAVE: At least you'll be able to listen like a virgin even though you look like a tart. (*Pause*) That bloody canal!

VICTORINE: You're going to lose every bloody franc you've got, I hope.

GUSTAVE: Everything.

FERDINAND: I bought some shares as well, not as many as Gustave, but enough.

BERTHE: Why?

FERDINAND: It was sold to us. We were persuaded.

GUSTAVE: I tell you—and don't pass this on—but most of the cash I'll get from father's will, when it's proved, is already in Suez shares. I borrowed up to the hilt on the strength of that money. . . .

VICTORINE: All that thrown in a ditch? You're mad.

GUSTAVE: Of course I'm mad.

FERDINAND: It's difficult to get at the truth. The papers can't be trusted because they're holding stock as well and they don't want to start a scare that will drive the price down. But we know that the labour, the Egyptians, don't want to carry on working on it. Why? You'd think with the way things are out there they'd be glad of the chance to earn some decent wages.

BERTHE: What kind of wages are they getting?

GUSTAVE: Not enough, if they've stopped work.

FERDINAND: That doesn't necessarily follow.

VICTORINE: Gustave, you put all that money into that company with your old man only dead a few weeks ago?

GUSTAVE: Well it's mine isn't it? I know it's there.

BERTHE: But sensible people don't take big decisions like that with the house in mourning. . . .

GUSTAVE: House in mourning. Me? You know how I feel. . . .

BERTHE: You are not *normal* when there's been a death, no one is. It alters things for a while. . . .

VICTORINE: You threw it away, Gustave, because it was burning a hole in your pocket. . . .

GUSTAVE: Nonsense. . . .

VICTORINE: Stupid tit. You should have given it to me.

GUSTAVE: They're not treating the native labour properly, that's obvious. Now they can do something about that. Make the work easier, pay better wages—I bet they get paid feathers— there is a way round the problem. But they won't do that, they must exploit them to the hilt, and destroy the whole scheme. That's what I can't understand.

FERDINAND: Well, we're shareholders, let's write to the company....

GUSTAVE: A lot of notice they'd take of us.

FERDINAND: It's our democratic right. We can go to the annual meeting....

GUSTAVE: The whole thing will be in ruins by then.

BERTHE: So what can you do?

FERDINAND: We have to trust in de Lesseps. We can't do anything.

BERTHE: It was a gamble, and you're losing. You've put nothing into it but money. Gustave, if you cared about that canal, then ... well, it would be different. If you were de Lesseps, or even the bloody Emperor, old fool that he is, then I might sympathize ... but you're not. You bet on a horse and it's stopped running. You're a mug to yourself.

GUSTAVE: Who was asking for sympathy?

BERTHE: You were. We've had this for days. I don't spend my time whining to you about my financial problems, do I? And I'm poor, Gustave, poor, really poor. Nothing is my own....

GUSTAVE: All right, all right....

BERTHE: When my father died there was nothing. Nothing. Except debts.

VICTORINE: Don't try and tell Gustave that he was lucky with his old man. He'll start screaming.

BERTHE: Look at all the things he did for you, good, solid things. You had a beautiful house in the country, apartments in Paris, holidays, respect at school from the grovelling teachers ... all this land, more houses with other people paying rent for you, for your legacy ... oho, Gustave, don't make me cry. His father was a saint, wasn't he, Victorine?

VICTORINE: Oh yes. When I saw him up there in the Palace of Justice looking down at me, I thought, there is a man who is close to God and all his holy angels. (*Pause*) On the way out I was picked up by Édouard who gave me twenty francs, took me to a friend's apartment and spent the afternoon teaching me the difference between the Old Testament and the New Testament.

FERDINAND: How is your mother, Gustave?

GUSTAVE: Underneath, happy I think. She puts on a face.

BERTHE: After all those years? Your mother feels right now as if her leg had been cut off.

GUSTAVE: I don't believe that.

BERTHE: She does. You be careful with her.

GUSTAVE: She won't stay in the house here. I think she'll sell it.

BERTHE: And give the money to you, you hope?

GUSTAVE: Édouard needs it as much as me.

VICTORINE: If I owned this land, I couldn't sell it. I thought you said it had been in the family for six hundred years? And you'd let her sell it?

GUSTAVE: I'd let her sell everything.

VICTORINE: That's stupid.

GUSTAVE: Why? I would make her free, and me free, and Édouard free. You want to try being chained to houses and fields and tenants. You can't cut yourself off from them. Why? Money. It's religious. Money is holy. It is the thing you pray to. Don't move. Don't think. Rest here, here's where the family money is. Sit on it. You can't escape.

VICTORINE: You don't want to anyway.

GUSTAVE: Oh yes I do.

VICTORINE: Then you can give me your share. I'll go and live with your mother. That would suit me fine.

GUSTAVE: I don't think it would fit in with her plans. Widowhood is supposed to be a tranquil time, sweetheart.

BERTHE: How much was the old man worth?

FERDINAND: Tut, tut. Watch your manners.

BERTHE: Why shouldn't I know? It's only a sum. Was he very well off when he died? Had he saved a lot?

GUSTAVE: Father was prudent. He was thinking of making it another hundred years that we'll be here, you see. We have to hold on, no matter what happens, we must have all this.

FERDINAND: And why not?

VICTORINE: Édouard, why not set me up here? Build a little house, put up a sign—Private. It's just what I need. I'd do some gardening, make my own clothes, bake bread. You promised me my own place. (*Pause*) See the crab smile? He's tighter than his old man was, the mean get!

FERDINAND: Victorine, if this was given to you, in a year it would be a jungle. You would neglect it, abuse it, the cattle would die. Land has to be loved and cared for . . . that's not your strong point.

VICTORINE: Cretin, I am a *part* of the landscape. Ask Édouard.

FERDINAND: Fun, that's you. For as long as you feel like. You're too wilful to be a farmer, or a lawyer. The old man was both, and good at it.

VICTORINE: You don't know that. If Édouard's father had been a woman from a poor family he might have ended up like me. We do what we have to. Now, if I had the chance, I could be very dependable, very solid and respectable. You don't believe me? I have friends who lived the same kind of life as me and Berthe do, then they married, settled down, and now they are so good and decent, children everywhere—children! And cooks? You've never tasted food like it. Their houses shine. You could eat your dinner off the floor. The same could be true of me.

GUSTAVE: I hope not.

VICTORINE: I could do it if I wanted to. It's not hard.

BERTHE: There's a housewife in every nymph, and in every lecher, Gustave, there's a little boy playing with himself under the bedclothes.

VICTORINE: Every tart I know would settle down if she could find a big-hearted, decent man. . . .

BERTHE: This one wouldn't. What happens after five years? He goes off you.

VICTORINE: Then you can go off him and do as you like—and you've got security, the priest will help you out if he starts talking about divorce—that's right out, my son, till death do you part—and you've got a couple of kids you've brought up on your side of the argument—a woman can't lose. You've got him! He has to give you money, you take what liberties you like and to hell with him. Let him get a tart of his own, leave you in peace.

GUSTAVE: Sounds wonderful, Victorine. Is this your plan?
VICTORINE: Yes. By the time I'm forty I've got to have it all set up. I'm just looking for the right man.
FERDINAND: I don't think Édouard would like to be considered. . . .
VICTORINE: I agree. He's not the type. I said he'd have to be big-hearted and decent before I could even think about exploiting him.
GUSTAVE: Yes, you did specify. Édouard, it seems you're out!
BERTHE: Not with me he isn't. Why do you keep me in the background Édouard? How you can fancy Victorine above me is . . . perplexing. Who admires you most? You are the sanest, most beautiful man I know. Ask me to share your life. I'll accept like a shot. We'll live quietly, intelligently, separated, together, married, unmarried. Do I mean it? (*Laughs*) NO!
GUSTAVE: He's cross. I can tell. You're not taking him seriously.
FERDINAND: You're wasting his money. Come on, let's start again. . . .
VICTORINE: Ferdy, shut up will you? I've been in and out of Édouard's studio all week, posing for him, working half the night. This is supposed to be my day off. If he doesn't know what I look like now, he never will.
FERDINAND: You are getting paid, Victorine. . . .
VICTORINE: Not much.
(*Pause*)
FERDINAND: It's what he can afford.
VICTORINE: Cha!
FERDINAND: He doesn't sell much at the moment. . . .
VICTORINE: And all that in the bank? Look Ferdy, he'll sell this. And why? Because I'm on it and I look good. Some old goat will buy it and stick it in his bedroom to get him going. Nobody's going to buy it because Édouard painted it.
FERDINAND: You better hadn't say that when he's listening. . . .
VICTORINE: He's always listening, and I've said it to him myself. I said it over coffee this morning and I'll say it over dinner tonight. I'm the one who's known, and I'm the stupid bitch who's poor.

(VICTORINE *stands up, wraps the cloak round her and walks down-stage.*)
GUSTAVE: Going to apologize?
VICTORINE: If I feel like it.
GUSTAVE: I know he beats you in private.
VICTORINE: You mean you hope he does. (*Pause*) Édouard, it feels odd. Are you sure it's the way you saw it? I mean, does it feel right to you? You're the one that matters. If you could only let me in on the secret—I did ask you last night but you didn't take any notice—what is the effect? (*Pause*) I'll be honest with you, I don't feel right . . . no, that's not the way I wanted to say that . . . I don't feel at ease. You're trying something out I know, but I'm the one people will be looking at and I'll be sitting there next to Gustave and Ferdy and they won't even be able to guess what we are supposed to be doing. It can't be just *new*. I could be saying to Gustave, pass me my dress. . . . Or Ferdy could be saying to me, did you cut my walking-stick in half? Or Berthe could be saying that she'd dropped her spectacles in the Seine. (*Pause*) Yes, I know you must experiment and we are all trying our hardest to understand, my love . . . couldn't you help us? Explain? Gustave and Ferdy will just look like . . .
FERDINAND: (*Going across to* VICTORINE) Victorine you should know better . . . leave him alone.
VICTORINE: . . . themselves, in their own clothes! And me? What about me?
FERDINAND: Édouard has given strict instructions. This is not going to be a bunfight, it is *work*. It has to be done properly. Leave him alone.
VICTORINE: I don't think he knows what he's doing.
FERDINAND: Nonsense! He's already given you a very definite form.
VICTORINE: The very definite form has been mine for years. He's making me look like a tart.
GUSTAVE: Angel, you *are* a tart.
VICTORINE: Not today I'm not. Today I'm a model. There's a difference. Édouard should know that.
(*Pause*)
FERDINAND: Victorine, he is after your essence.

VICTORINE: Drink is it now?
FERDINAND: Édouard isn't interested in the false ideas you've got about yourself, or any pretensions. He's trying to find you, the real original you . . . the divine animal in its own time.
VICTORINE: Mooooooo! Ticktockticktockticktock. Mooooooo!
FERDINAND: We are what we are, Victorine. You're not ashamed of it, are you? What do you want to see in the painting?
VICTORINE: Not what I can see in any mirror. He should be improving me.
FERDINAND: You mean telling lies?
VICTORINE: All right, yes. What I *might* be, what I *could* be—but what's the point of doing me as I am? I'm here, there it is. Who needs two of me? I don't, you don't.
FERDINAND: Look, all I'm trying to do is keep the conditions right so he can make his experiment. . . .
BERTHE: Ferdy, you don't let on do you? You keep everything to yourself. Why the hell didn't you tell us that Édouard had changed his job, given up painting altogether and decided to be a scientist? It would have helped us divine little white mice no end if we'd known. We'd have behaved ourselves much better, wouldn't we? Of course we would, quite naturally. Me, now I'd stay in my cage, tearing round my treadmill, making eyes at Ferdinand, the handsome, manly laboratory cat.
FERDINAND: You're very unfair.
BERTHE: Pusspusspusspuss.
FERDINAND: Try and understand will you?
BERTHE: Perhaps we do, too well. We do have minds of our own, you know.
FERDINAND: There must be a period when everything is in place for him, when he can have order to work from.
GUSTAVE: What's the matter with *dis*order, Ferdy? A good disorder is just as useful any day, and much more interesting. You see, Berthe, my love, you've got it all wrong. Édouard is a painter *and* a scientist. He will shortly paint a cure for cholera, wave it in front of Egypt's diseased millions and they will be well again, well enough to return to the diggings and the excavation of my investment. So, for Doctor

Édouard we must keep the laboratory conditions stable on both counts. Oh God, the river is rising! We have prior warning of an earthquake. The test-tubes are trembling! The pipettes are positively pixillating!

BERTHE: The germs are escaping! Come back you bad bastards!

VICTORINE: They're getting in the paint! They're crawling on the canvas! I can hear them screaming—we're stuck! We're stuck!

GUSTAVE: Still life of typhus. Side view of smallpox. The plague, reclining nude with a background of Paris.

VICTORINE: And this gallery isn't big enough for Édouard's scientific pictures, is it? He's got to work on a large scale to say all he's got to say, hasn't he? Knock down that wall. Take off the roof. Ferdy, don't let the public get closer than ten paces or the picture will melt away into dots and numbers. Oh, and the light must be right. What time should we ask them to come round for the viewing?

BERTHE: Oh, dawn, dawn, definitely dawn. They can bring their breakfasts.

VICTORINE: What's this? You've been boozing! Smoking what? Opium! If you come in here, mate, the only inspiration you're supposed to get is from me! And you . . . you've just walked from Rheims? Had sex, a heavy dinner, come off the night shift? Get out of here. You're in no fit state to see what Édouard Manet makes of the world as it is today! What are you missing? What's the mystery? Well, it's a picture of an unadorned tart whose ears stick out. You'll give it a miss after all? Pity. You seem the perfect man to see this masterpiece—you're so normal, sir, which should give you a taste for abnormality. Five francs. Oh no, that's not the entry fee, that's the cost of this canvas—it's one of the new photographs! CHARLATAN!

(*Pause*)

GUSTAVE: Édouard, I warned you about using a model who can draw herself. She expects some element of flattering transformation. Now, you should be able to manage that. You were trained for a naval career so telling lies to women should come easy to you.

VICTORINE: I don't want a lie, you ape—I just want something of the best part of me . . . I'm leaving. That's it!
FERDINAND: You can't!
VICTORINE: Try and stop me!
FERDINAND: Please, Victorine . . . I implore you.
VICTORINE: I feel better now you're begging. You are doing it for Édouard aren't you? Even at one step removed, it's sweet. There. I'll stay for you, you old groveller.
GUSTAVE: He's done it again. Without saying a word he has changed another mind. He did the same with father. He had Édouard marked down for a naval career. It's true, it's true. Off he went in his uniform, looking very bright and blue, and was shipped off in a training vessel to South America. He hated it. Why? Now, Édouard, what is the difference between a line here—we'll say this one, from Victorine's divine coccyx, the stump of the monkey's tail . . . to the nape of her exquisite neck (beneath the shadow of her ears) . . . and a line of latitude from Le Havre to Rio de Janeiro? Cannot a sailor paint? Or a painter sail? From that time in his tormented adolescence Édouard has been on eternal shore-leave.
VICTORINE: Boozing. Whoring.
BERTHE: Having a gay old time before his next voyage of discovery.
VICTORINE: The man who can only look in the mirror. The black box with the pin-hole in it. The man on the tripod who must remain still while the image registers. Before long we'll have no need for painters. They'll all be out of business.
FERDINAND: That could be caused by their models moving about so often they can't get any work done.
GUSTAVE: Father bought him out of his apprenticeship, allowed Édouard to talk him into sending him to old Couture's studio . . . a tremendous act of adolescent persuasion! How did you do it? It could have been blackmail. What did you threaten? Suicide?
FERDINAND: Édouard could not stop himself being a painter.
GUSTAVE: Could I stop myself becoming a doctor?
FERDINAND: You seem to be managing so far.

GUSTAVE: I was *told* I would be a doctor, Édouard chose. . . .
FERDINAND: No. He was chosen.
GUSTAVE: Ferdy, what a slave you are.
FERDINAND: Perhaps.
(*Pause*)
BERTHE: I'm getting hungry.
VICTORINE: How about some food, Ferdy? Are we allowed to eat now?
GUSTAVE: Édouard, you should have had some success as a painter before the old man died. He needed to know that he'd done the right thing, like a judge who gets a confession from the prisoner after the sentence. That would have been nice for him. As it is, Édouard, you haven't made it yet.
FERDINAND: He will.
BERTHE: I hope so.
GUSTAVE: I don't doubt it. I'm just thinking of our father, poor man, dying in doubt. That, for a gentleman of the Second Empire, must be like hanging over hell on a bar of butter.
VICTORINE: You'll get a rotten face put on you in this one, Gustave.
BERTHE: No, not Édouard. There's no vindictiveness there. (*Nestles up to* FERDINAND.) Warm me up, Ferdy.
VICTORINE: Édouard, we're going to have something to eat now. Come on over.
BERTHE: I bet he's put a backside on me like a carthorse. Now, Édouard, this lunch here—(*Touches the overturned basket right.*)—we don't eat this lunch.
GUSTAVE: That lunch is not a real lunch. That lunch is Édouard's lunch.
BERTHE: Ferdy, be a good lad and get the genuine lunch out of the boat. . . .
GUSTAVE: The authentic boat!
BERTHE: Which is floating. . . .
GUSTAVE: Real trees! Real sky! Real autumn! Real water! Real ripples!
BERTHE: On the sincere Seine!
(FERDINAND *gets up and goes to the boat for the lunch-basket.*)
GUSTAVE: Victorine, give Édouard a smile.

20

VICTORINE: (*Smiling*) There. (*Pause*) He ignores it.
GUSTAVE: You know why?
VICTORINE: I'm not trying hard enough. (*Smiles*) Ah, a flicker. Look, he's showing me his eye-teeth.
GUSTAVE: He loves you.
VICTORINE: He loves us all. Ferdy's sister, me on Mondays, Wednesdays and week-ends. Mimi-the-Breton on Tuesday, Eggs-On-a-Plate on Thursday. . . .
FERDINAND: Shut up, Victorine.
(*Pause.* FERDINAND *starts unpacking the basket.*)
BERTHE: You're talking yourself out of a job.
VICTORINE: I'll manage.
GUSTAVE: My girl, to Édouard you are a pot of pink paint.
BERTHE: That's not true. He's very fond of Victorine.
(*Pause. They lay out the picnic.*)
VICTORINE: Édouard, come and have something to eat.
GUSTAVE: Don't bother. . . .
VICTORINE: (*Sharply*) No! He must have something! He can't go on like this . . . Édouard, you must eat!
GUSTAVE: You sound like Mother. Victorine, Édouard is not eating these days. You know why. So why not leave him alone?
(*Pause*)
VICTORINE: I notice that you still have a healthy appetite Gustave.
GUSTAVE: My stomach has not gone into mourning. And you notice his insistence that it was a picnic he is painting. He will paint the idea of eating, but will not eat himself. Further, there have to be *two* lunch-baskets . . . don't you find that tantalizing? (*Kisses* VICTORINE.)
VICTORINE: He's watching.
BERTHE: What a bore you are, Gustave. You try so hard.
GUSTAVE: There's no harm. It is not a real kiss. It is one ghost kissing another. (*Kisses* VICTORINE *again.*) And that was a reflection, a ripple effect. (*Kisses her again.*) And that was an echo, Narcissus.
VICTORINE: Édouard, I can never trust your eyes. They say everything I don't want them to say. You've got an

animal's eyes.
GUSTAVE: She's mine. (*Kisses* VICTORINE *again.*) I'm the one who's sitting next to her in the pose. You put me there. (*Kisses her again.*) This is the potential, what could happen. Now put that in as well. (*To* FERDINAND, *harshly.*) How old is Léon now?
FERDINAND: Oh . . . er . . . about ten I should think. Yes, about ten.
VICTORINE: See if I care. Why should I? Great ponce, he is.
GUSTAVE: And his mother, Suzanne? Still playing the piano?
FERDINAND: Be quiet, Gustave.
GUSTAVE: If I had a son I would own him.
BERTHE: If you had a son you would die of fright.
FERDINAND: It is their business Gustave. Suzanne has made no complaint.
GUSTAVE: Of course not. She feels privileged. Now I would like a son but there's no one who'll bear me one. God, I would own him, be proud of him. Édouard, I will take him from you and raise him. Tell your sister, Ferdy, that you have found a home for the boy. We will go out to the Suez Canal and dig it together. We will save the economy of France, uncle and natural nephew. (*Waves*) Yes, I'll get married, Édouard, do it all myself and it will be nothing to do with you. I am jealous that you can have a bastard and no one minds, no one. It's wonderful!
VICTORINE: Your mother managed it with little fuss.
GUSTAVE: Oh, cruel!
BERTHE: One day you will push Édouard too far, then God help you.
GUSTAVE: No, he would help Édouard.
FERDINAND: I'll get the rest of the wine. It should be nice and cool by now.
(FERDINAND *goes over to the boat and takes two bottles of white wine from under a stone in the water, then brings them back.* BERTHE *takes out a newspaper and opens it.* FERDINAND *wipes the bottles.*)
Will we drink them both fairly quickly?
BERTHE: Is that an invitation?

FERDINAND: If we're not going to then I'll put one of them back.

GUSTAVE: He worked that all out for himself you know.

(FERDINAND *goes back to the boat and puts one bottle back under the stone in the water.* GUSTAVE *opens the other.*)

BERTHE: Mexico, Mexico, Mexico, Mexico . . . (*Shuts the paper suddenly.*) Where is Mexico? What are we doing in Mexico?

GUSTAVE: In Mexico there is a snow-capped mountain, a volcano called Popocatepetl, which is shaped like a warrior kneeling at the feet of his sleeping sweetheart. That is all I know about Mexico.

FERDINAND: (*Returning*) Mexico owes us money. She owes England money. If we don't do something to recover the debts . . . Mexico will renege. . . .

BERTHE: Mexico is America. The Emperor is saying Mexico is in France. He is a terrible old fool and I would cut his balls off with an axe. After all we've been through we are still sending French soldiers to America, still. Shit! (*She crumples the paper up into a ball and pounds it together.*) It makes me ashamed! And you do as well! (*She hurls the paper ball at* FERDINAND *who hurls it back.*) What's happened to us? We're going backwards.

FERDINAND: America? There is no America? They're tearing each other to pieces. The continent is completely unstable. The civil war is killing it.

BERTHE: Over slavery, you fool! Mexico is not in France! Where is it? It is in Mexico! And Louis Napoléon expects us to care. . . .

GUSTAVE: (*Pouring out the wine*) Now, I have a solution to the problem of slavery. If the two sides in the United States would pause for a breather, put all their black people in boats and send them over to dig the Suez Canal, we would have peace on one hand, and prosperity on the other. Will anyone drink to that?

BERTHE: Édouard, if you ever paint the Emperor, or his stooge Maximilian, I'll pour all your paints down your throat and poison you! Well, don't you think it's vile, Victorine? Trying to put a congenital cretin like that old Habsburg Maximilian on the throne in a *new* country?

GUSTAVE: Don't ask her. She doesn't understand. There, there. Drink your wine, my child. Now, Berthe, you have the wrong attitude. Maximilian will pay debts to France and introduce the drinking of schnapps to replace tequila, street-rioting to replace bull-fighting—infinitely more fun— and the Folies Bergère to oust the fandango. I mean, do we need another civilization when we have this one? They won't be able to do anything better than we can. Let them use our expertise, our experience.

BERTHE: We will pay for it, like we paid for betraying our own revolution, not once but twice! Look at us . . . it makes you want to cry.

GUSTAVE: But we're very good at making emperors. The ones we make are nothing but the best. I mean, look at the Dutch . . . I know you'll forgive me Ferdy . . . how much better they would be for some really royal encrustations. Now Ferdy, I am prepared to sell you Louis Napoléon in exchange for a waggon-load of tulip bulbs. Don't hesitate. The next time your country is in any danger of flooding you will only have to send him up on the top of the dykes and the water will calm. It's a knack he has. What do you say?

FERDINAND: Of course. I'll arrange it immediately. (*Walks down-stage.*)

VICTORINE: I don't know why you let yourself get so upset, Berthe. . . .

BERTHE: It is me who is being made a fool! Me! You stick an old goat like the Emperor on me! I'm disgusted! France is finished!

FERDINAND: Édouard, I hope you've been able to get some work done. Things have not been exactly perfect. Yes, I try. You're patient, I wish I were like you but I feel like beating him about the head sometimes. . . .

VICTORINE: Berthe, he will die . . . the old goat will die.

BERTHE: When? I'll tell you, innocent, when I'm an old tart and you're an old tart and we won't give a damn who is in the government!

FERDINAND: Although Suzanne doesn't object to Victorine, and never will . . . whether it's her or . . . someone else . . . it has to be said before the wedding, that she doesn't want you to expect her to come to the studio or on jaunts like this. This will be your province. She will never interfere, or ask for explanations. Suzanne knows what kind of life you must lead in order to find what you want . . . but there are risks, you know.

VICTORINE: Who says I'm going to be an old tart?

BERTHE: Of course you are. It can't be helped. We all are. All I'm saying is that I don't want France making me a ridiculous old tart before my time!

FERDINAND: And Édouard, I'd like us to find time to talk about Léon. He knows you're his father but unless you do something about it soon he's not going to respect that relationship. His attitude is this—if you won't accept him, and only accept his mother . . . well, then he's an orphan. Those are his own words. He's a bright boy but I feel that hollowness, you know, that brittleness growing. He's just surface glitter.

BERTHE: I'll prove to you that you're going to be an old tart. Gustave, would you marry her?

GUSTAVE: Certainly not.

BERTHE: You know why?

GUSTAVE: Because I'm hopelessly in love with her.

BERTHE: Ah, how sad.

GUSTAVE: You understand?

BERTHE: Perfectly.

GUSTAVE: The Emperor is the man who started this fashion. He loves France, so he abuses her. Édouard loves Suzanne, Léon, Victorine, etcetera . . . so he is cruel to them. I worship Victorine but will not share my life with her . . . though we have things in common, don't we?

VICTORINE: Unfortunately.

GUSTAVE: Thus we get along. We can share a cup without wiping the rim.

(*Pause*)

FERDINAND: Getting back to your . . . material interests Gustave, what is really upsetting you: the Emperor is the only person who will get the Suez Canal completed. He'll send the

Foreign Legion in to finish it off before he'll let the Egyptians lose all your money for you.

GUSTAVE: That is very kind of the old fellow. However, my gratitude is mixed with resentment. Do you know who it was that made me buy fifty five-hundred-franc shares in a hole in the sand? The Emperor. He is the teacher who taught me to waste my resources, to spend dead men's money, and to be greedy. So, my feelings towards him are ambiguous. On the one hand I hate him and on the other I loathe his guts.

VICTORINE: Gustave, you're lazy. That is your fault, no one else's.

GUSTAVE: True.

VICTORINE: When did you last do any work on your studies?

GUSTAVE: Weeks ago.

VICTORINE: Was it the Emperor who kept dragging you into cafés and dance-halls and pouring drink down your throat?

GUSTAVE: I have been trying to forget that his name is Napoléon and that the only battle he has ever won has been against Frenchmen.

(*Pause*)

VICTORINE: You are what you are. You don't really want to be a doctor.

GUSTAVE: No, get it right. I don't want to be a quack. (*Pause*) Why did my father not buy any canal stock, not a solitary share? Did you know that? Paris went mad when they opened trading in those shares. You couldn't get near the Exchange I hear. But he wouldn't touch it.

FERDINAND: Which is why you did.

GUSTAVE: Talk sense will you?

FERDINAND: Your father saved. You want to make money fast.

GUSTAVE: What's wrong with that? Do I want to die with it?

VICTORINE: Too damn right. Show me how.

FERDINAND: Only so you can be as rich as your father *before* Édouard. That's the key.

BERTHE: Ah-ha.

GUSTAVE: Well, what a revelation. Do I really?

FERDINAND: Rivalry is at the root of it.

GUSTAVE: For rivalry read revelry. I've never heard such rubbish. See, even Édouard is laughing.

FERDINAND: There is always a reason, and sometimes it's a dark one, deep inside yourself. You want to get there before Édouard. You compete with him in everything you do or say.

(*Pause*)

VICTORINE: So there.

BERTHE: That's you fixed up.

FERDINAND: If you could, by some miracle, become an absolute replica of your father tomorrow, you'd do it.

GUSTAVE: And sleep with my mother, I suppose?

VICTORINE: I doubt if she'd notice the difference.

GUSTAVE: And I thought I was the one who always looked up to Édouard, who followed him around. Hear that comrade? It wasn't that I wanted to be like you, I wanted to be better—cheaply. Well, Ferdy, my biography is yours. I give you full rights to print it. Christ in Heaven, you know it all!

(*Pause*)

VICTORINE: How do you know all that about Gustave? Are you guessing?

FERDINAND: Oh no, I'm not that perceptive. Édouard told me.

(*Pause*)

BERTHE: Hm. Anyone want to share a melon?

GUSTAVE: Édouard said that?

FERDINAND: Yes.

BERTHE: Did he tell it to you in confidence?

FERDINAND: No. He said everyone knew it anyway but he was just expressing it.

BERTHE: He's taken his brother to bits and seen what's wrong with him?

FERDINAND: No, how he *is*. That's his real gift. He can cut through. Édouard has a very clear vision of the truth. He knows Gustave's truth.

VICTORINE: Well, good old Édouard. God knows what he must think of me. What an opinion to have about yourself. It's not unlike the good God.

FERDINAND: It's not an opinion, it's a fact. He can get outside and look in . . . it's a mechanism, a quirk, the way his mind is built. Fascinating.

VICTORINE: I'll keep my eye on him in future. He never told me he was God.

(*Pause.* GUSTAVE *gets to his feet, walks down-stage.*)

GUSTAVE: Édouard . . . er . . . I have a suggestion to make . . . no, no, not about the work in hand . . . no, it's about a holiday we must take together. We have never been to the Dordogne you know, never. That is something we must remedy. We'll go to the Dordogne and we'll go to the prehistoric caves and we'll stand side by side and look at the paintings which men *had* to do in their brothers' blood because they had no better materials. And, you know, the world has yet to produce a painter to beat them. Go on, paint me an animal that lives, my Paris café caveman, let's see you wield your bison bristles at Tortini's tomorrow, real flesh, real animals. ME! What else have you been saying about me? ME? You are the one who wants success and you'll do anything for it. If I want to beat you to it, that's just a race between two men, but you? You want to lick the whole earth, have its neck in your claws, Mr Gentleman. You want genuine, sincere greed? There it is, looking exquisitely reasonable, poised, unconcerned; the human glacier rubbing the rocks down to make his going easier. I am not in competition with you. I can't paint. I can't sculpt like Ferdy, I can't even make a living out of friendship like the girls . . . so where's the challenge? You want to match me for losing money?

(VICTORINE *comes over to* GUSTAVE *and holds him.*)

VICTORINE: Gustave, you're drunk. Don't shout at Édouard.

GUSTAVE: He must stop being so critical of me! I didn't ask for it!

VICTORINE: He's not critical. He says that's the way you are, that's all. . . .

GUSTAVE: And who is he to say so? A dauber? A dilettante? Let him go and suffer and then paint, smug sod . . . it's all rotten. He doesn't have to . . .

(VICTORINE *leads* GUSTAVE *back to the picnic.*)

. . . no, there's no *necessity* for him to paint. He's got his private income, so he'll never be an honest painter. He plays with it . . . God if I only had a job! And you, you bloody know-all! You wait. I'll end up a better tart's doctor than you'll be a painter. I'll cure them, you won't!

(VICTORINE *sits down and pillows* GUSTAVE's *head on her lap, taps him.*)

VICTORINE: Shut up and I'll let you make love to my ears.
GUSTAVE: Yes, and you'll give Édouard the rest.
VICTORINE: Give? Never.
GUSTAVE: Go on, we know.
VICTORINE: Édouard always has his hand in his pocket for me, don't you?

(*Pause*)

FERDINAND: (*Swatting something on his cheek*) Get off!
BERTHE: I thought all the flies should be dead by now. Bastards!

(*An attack of flies. While* VICTORINE, BERTHE *and* FERDINAND *are busy swatting them, driving them away from the food,* GUSTAVE *lifts up his face and holds out his hands.*)

GUSTAVE: Come on, come on, give me a kiss. Straight off the dung. Come on.
FERDINAND: Bloody filthy things! Get away!
VICTORINE: They're after the meat. (*Covers it up.*)
GUSTAVE: Get them all in, Édouard. Don't forget the flies. There's one, there's another. Now look at that, they won't land on me. What's the matter with me? Come on, you lads, free space here, plenty of room.
BERTHE: Leave them for a minute. Let them settle.

(*They stop moving, watching the flies.*)

GUSTAVE: Édouard, I have even been rejected by the flies. How can I be a good doctor now? We all need friends, brother.
BERTHE: GO!

(FERDINAND, VICTORINE *and* BERTHE *swat flies all round the picnic in a furious assault. Pause.*)

GUSTAVE: In the name of the Father, Son and Holy Ghost, Amen.
FERDINAND: Well, I'm not eating that now. . . .
VICTORINE: Don't be stupid. Flies never killed anybody.
FERDINAND: You please yourself. Just think what they've been

walking in.

BERTHE: Ferdy, you've got to die sometime.

VICTORINE: In Africa they eat flies. (*Picking flies off the picnic.*) How about that?

GUSTAVE: As a fly-killer, I'm a failure. As a fly-lover, I'm a failure.

VICTORINE: Well, you can try to be a good doctor. That would be helpful.

(*Pause*)

GUSTAVE: Édouard will have seventy thousand francs, I repeat, seventy thousand francs! when the old man's affairs are all settled. Why do you bother to paint, Édouard? You don't need to earn a living. . . .

FERDINAND: He could not stop if he wanted to. It's in his blood.

GUSTAVE: Then it should be in mine as well. But it isn't. Perhaps there isn't room in mine.

FERDINAND: You will feel a fool one day Gustave. When Édouard is given the gold medal, when his work is hung in the Louvre in his own lifetime, when they make him a Chevalier d'Honneur, you will regret this attitude.

GUSTAVE: I am going to discontinue my studies.

VICTORINE: You are the only man I know who can stop what he never started.

GUSTAVE: Who needs a quack with my brother around? He can do a doctor's job. You've lost your nose? Whip round to his studio, sit still for a while, caramba! Hey presto! New nose! Not only a new nose, but a nose of genius.

(*Distant shouts and whistles off, very faint.*)

He could reconstruct the ancient face of Paris. You, Berthe, could have a pair of Victorine's ears. . . .

BERTHE: I'll stick to my own if it's all right with you.

GUSTAVE: And Victorine could have a pair of Berthe's breasts for state occasions and funerals. It's a marvellous idea. Édouard, we should form a company and issue shares in your talent now!

FERDINAND: Gustave. . . .

GUSTAVE: Édouard could paint over every defect he sees in us. It would be a new world. Girls, buy shares in Édouard at

once!
FERDINAND: Will you please. . . .
GUSTAVE: He is the canvas Christ. He can make us all entirely waterproof.
(*Pause*)
FERDINAND: Apologize, quickly!
GUSTAVE: Sorry, Édouard. I got carried away with my own enthusiasm. Just one last request. When you re-paint the boulevards of the city, will you widen them a little so we can get your head along in the procession to the investiture ceremony.
BERTHE: (*Laughing*) Édouard, give him at least a black look!
FERDINAND: You're being a disruptive influence, Gustave. . . .
BERTHE: Oh don't be so solemn, Ferdy!
VICTORINE: Berthe is enjoying herself.
BERTHE: Oh dear.
VICTORINE: You want Édouard? Go and get him. He doesn't belong to me.
BERTHE: He can take a joke, I know that much. Gustave is always like this with him. Why be so sensitive?
VICTORINE: Because this picture is going to be . . . shit. I know it. You won't take him seriously, Gustave hates him . . . he gets thrown.
BERTHE: Nonsense. He knows every move he makes.
VICTORINE: You ask him now whether he can paint or not. He doubts himself. He doesn't know why he's put this picture together like this. He's groping. . . .
GUSTAVE: All right, we're groping with him aren't we?
FERDINAND: You don't want him to succeed though, do you, Gustave?
(*Pause*. GUSTAVE *turns away, sinks down in* VICTORINE'*s lap*.)
BERTHE: Ferdy, don't be so ham-fisted with Gustave again. It puts me off you for a long time.
FERDINAND: He knows what I'm talking about. He's perfectly aware of what's the matter with him.
(GUSTAVE *starts to snore loudly*. VICTORINE *strokes his head*.)
BERTHE: And what is that? I mean, that's different to the rest of us.

FERDINAND: He's jealous of Édouard.
  (GUSTAVE *increases the volume of his snoring.*)
VICTORINE: The baby has dropped off. Now we can have some peace.
BERTHE: (*Touching* VICTORINE) Sweetheart, I don't want him, honestly. Have I ever tried to take a man away from you? Besides, I don't think I'm that good. . . . (*Kisses her.*) All right? I tell you, Édouard will do a powerful job on this one, I know it. . . .
VICTORINE: I shouldn't have snapped . . . but I am worried. I cannot bear to think of him being confused. . . .
  (*A bearded man—*HUGO—*suddenly erupts out of the river, spouting water, exhaling air.*)
FERDINAND: (*Jumping up*) Hey, get out of here! Get out! This is private property!
BERTHE: (*Laughing*) It's a river-god, Édouard! Just what you need!
VICTORINE: (*Pushing* GUSTAVE *off her lap*) Come on out! Oh, look at him, he's out of breath . . . give him a hand.
FERDINAND: Go on, shove off, you've no right here. . . .
VICTORINE: O shut up, Ferdy! Hey you, come and join us. . . .
BERTHE: Don't send him away! Ask him over. . . .
FERDINAND: Girls, you're ruining Édouard's afternoon . . . how is he going to paint with strangers here?
VICTORINE: Who cares? The pictures not going to work anyway.
FERDINAND: Get out man! Go on! (*He raises his cane at* HUGO *as he wades out of the water.*) This is not a public bathing-place. You're trespassing. . . .
  (HUGO, *who is a swarthy, powerfully-built, shaggy character, grabs the cane and throws it away, still puffing and spitting water and wringing out his beard. He wears a tattered white pair of underpants.*)
HUGO: A hundred! I held my breath for a hundred.
FERDINAND: Édouard, for God's sake help me.
BERTHE: Welcome, river-god. Stop and recline a while. Édouard, got a pose for him? Can you handle a trident?
VICTORINE: Come and sit down. Here's a towel, dry yourself.
  (*She throws him a towel. Then she sees* HUGO's *boils for the*

32

first time. They are on his thighs.)

HUGO: Sorry. I won't use your towel. . . .

VICTORINE: Go ahead. You're amongst friends.

FERDINAND: Look, let me explain . . . sir, we are having a picture painted . . . you are intruding. . . .

VICTORINE: Give him some wine, Ferdy.

(VICTORINE *and* BERTHE *rub* HUGO *dry with the towel.* FERDINAND *unwillingly pours out a glass of wine, walks down-stage.*)

FERDINAND: Why don't you say something, Édouard? If you don't mind then I don't . . . the girls are just being awkward for the sake of it . . . they're bored I think. I'll let him stay for a couple of minutes then get rid of him. . . .

HUGO: I would like to rest for a moment. I won't disturb you much longer. I ran out of breath and got frightened.

BERTHE: You swim late in the season.

HUGO: It is supposed to be good for me, the mineral salts in the water heal my boils . . . so my doctor says.

VICTORINE: Well, what is your name. Ferdy is too upset to introduce us.

FERDINAND: (*Giving the wine to* HUGO) Not at all. Édouard does not seem to mind our visitor being here, so I can be as polite as naturally I would prefer to be. Forgive me, sir. I was protecting my friend's valuable working-time. I hope you will understand.

HUGO: Completely. Excuse my disrespect to your stick. (*He picks up the cane and returns it to* FERDINAND *with a smile.*)

FERDINAND: Now, we are composed again. At your feet, sir . . . is Monsieur Gustave Manet. He is not circulating in society today. So, an explanation of his presence rather than an introduction. This is Mademoiselle Victorine Meurent. . . .

HUGO: Enchanté. My name is Moor.

VICTORINE: Moor? You have a first name?

BERTHE: It would be very difficult to call a river-god Moor.

HUGO: Hugo Moor.

FERDINAND: Then, Hugo, this is Mademoiselle Berthe Peudefrat.

HUGO: Enchanté.

BERTHE: Hello, Hugo Moor.

(*Pause*)

HUGO: And your name, sir?

FERDINAND: Ferdinand Leenhoff.

BERTHE: Call him Ferdy like we do.

HUGO: Sir. (*Bows*)

BERTHE: Have you had any lunch?

HUGO: Thank you, but I cannot join you. It is dangerous to swim on a full stomach and I must return to the other bank shortly. But I am enjoying this excellent wine. May I ask the name of the painter who is so busy?

VICTORINE: That is Édouard Manet, the brother of this thing here. It's all right, don't scratch your head, you've never heard of him.

HUGO: That is true, but then he has never heard of me. Neither of us need feel ashamed. What is this picture?

FERDINAND: I think he will call it 'The Bathers' or something like that. It's an idyllic, pastoral thing. You know what I mean. Victorine here is naked, Berthe is in the river, Gustave and I are just sitting around doing nothing in particular . . . talking, I suppose.

HUGO: You are models?

VICTORINE: Yes.

HUGO: Do you think he is a good painter?

VICTORINE: I don't know.

HUGO: Does he?

VICTORINE: Oh yes. He knows he's good.

HUGO: That is what matters. To me that sounds like a strong man.

BERTHE: But what if he isn't any good?

HUGO: Then it will be painful for him finding out. But as he is a strong man, he will survive it. I hope I'm not disturbing him too much.

VICTORINE: He's not batting an eyelid.

GUSTAVE: (*Still with his eyes closed*) Now, I'm going to guess what the river-god looks like. I haven't seen him, only heard his voice. You're all a witness to that. I am going to give you a full, accurate description of this river-god purely from his voice, the sounds he has made, and the thoughts he has expressed. Would anyone care to make a bet that I can't do it?

HUGO: Ah, the sleeper awakes.

GUSTAVE: Shamming, I'm afraid. I do a lot of shamming. I sham all sorts of ailments, but my speciality is breakdowns. I can break down at a moment's notice. Now, no bets? Come on, this isn't easy you know. Think of all the possibilities. I don't know whether he's tall, or short . . . anything, only the voice . . . ten francs anyone? Five? (*He stands up, back to* HUGO.)

HUGO: I will pay you five francs for the entertainment, but I will have to send it to you. Go on. It will be fun.

GUSTAVE: Are you all satisfied that I have not looked at this river-god at all? That I am working only with my imagination, and my intelligence . . . hear this Édouard? And *my* sensitivity! And sixth sense!

VICTORINE: He must be talking about someone else.

GUSTAVE: The river-god has told me only two things about himself: that he has boils—I apologize for raising that; and that he likes to test himself—his underwater counting; ah, three, he disarmed Ferdy with little effort; four, he apologized; five, he did not give his first name; six, he likes good wine. . . . Hugo, you have told me so many things but how does that help me make a *real* picture of you? What do you look like? I'll tell you river-god. (*Pause*) You are a golden myth, a dream with a disease. You are as much a myth as Zeus, and Aphrodite—she's sitting next to you, that pale, hairless thing like a Mexican dog—ears and all. It's all a myth, except money. Fat and false and filthy and French. And here we are in this beautiful world, talking to men we have not seen.

(*Pause.* GUSTAVE *remains with his back to* HUGO, *then puts out a hand.* HUGO *takes it.* GUSTAVE *smiles. They hold the handclasp. Lights fade to Blackout.*)

ACT TWO

GUSTAVE *and* HUGO *in the handclasp,* GUSTAVE *still with his eyes shut.*

GUSTAVE: Good man.
HUGO: If you're going to look at me now, brace yourself. I'm a terrible sight.
GUSTAVE: Is it that bad?
BERTHE: Don't believe him, Gustave. He's a fine figure of a man.
GUSTAVE: Ssh! Don't demote him. He's a river-god, Berthe. (*Pause*) When I open my eyes, however you look, I'm going to like you. Yes, I'm going to do that on trust. For as long as you are here, I'm going to like you, and have faith in you, river-god.
VICTORINE: Hugo, you are suddenly in a lot of trouble.
HUGO: It will be a risky business? Well, what else is life for? Sir, don't expect too much. I'm only a poor man.
GUSTAVE: Oh stay a myth and make some money. (*Opens his eyes.*) There! You're just as I thought. You look the same as your voice sounds.
HUGO: I'll have to think about whether that is a compliment or not.
GUSTAVE: You are everything I expected. Édouard, look at this. Now here is a chance for me to be helpful. I know a secret. You have taken the positions in the picture from Gorgione, who took them from Raphael, who took them from some tombs in Rome. You don't deny it, you can't, I saw the sketches. Now, in the original, was a river-god, sitting like Ferdy is supposed to be, and naked. So, give Ferdy the elbow and substitute this splendid specimen who has just beached himself here by a stroke of great good luck! Ferdy is taking the whole thing far too seriously anyway. (*Pause*)

36

At least think about it. Go on, put him in the picture—
Hugo, I regret to say that you have been rejected.

HUGO: How humiliating.

GUSTAVE: Now you have no function. You are useless.

HUGO: I am thoroughly ashamed of myself.

GUSTAVE: Would you like the loan of a razor?

(*Pause.* HUGO *laughs and puts an arm round* GUSTAVE's *shoulder.* GUSTAVE *smiles then abruptly pushes* HUGO *away and points an accusing finger.*)

What are you doing here?

HUGO: Pardon?

GUSTAVE: You should be back in Egypt, working on the canal.

HUGO: I should?

GUSTAVE: If you think you can desert your post, throw away your shovel and come to Paris to find more profitable employment, you are mistaken! You must return to the diggings at once, in chains! Swim back!

HUGO: I will have to think about it.

GUSTAVE: No time. What does the tribunal say?

BERTHE: Well, even if he doesn't go, his pants will have to. I'm not prepared to see the fashions altered to suit them. Victorine would look dreadful in those, wouldn't you, darling? What a sight.

VICTORINE: Have you got black blood in you?

HUGO: No.

GUSTAVE: Liar! Lowest of the lowest fellaheen! Do you eat flies?

VICTORINE: You're very dark. Berthe likes dark men.

HUGO: (*Bowing*) Then I am content.

FERDINAND: Forgive them. We can't do anything about their manners when we hire them. This is all sport.

HUGO: I had seen that a long time ago. It is good to laugh so soon with new people.

(*Pause*)

GUSTAVE: Well, the kindest thing said today. For that he must be excused his pants.

(VICTORINE *gives* HUGO's *pants a tug as if to pull them off. He sheers away.*)

FERDINAND: Victorine! Enough! Behave yourself.

VICTORINE: I just wanted to be sure he wasn't the Bearded Lady from the circus.

GUSTAVE: We are prepared to turn a blind eye to the fact that you are an escaped labourer from the Suez Canal—no doubt the company are scouring the desert for you right now—providing, and you must swear to this, that you do not own a single share of stock in that ridiculous enterprise.

HUGO: Not a one.

GUSTAVE: Promise?

HUGO: On my oath.

GUSTAVE: I would have to withdraw every kind word I've said about you if I discovered that you were as big a fool as I am. Now these people have not taken you into their hearts like I have—but they will. These girls are trained to take strangers into their bosoms with immense speed, and this man will attack you with a chisel if you stand still long enough. They are all of them mad. You're mad!

HUGO: Is he talking to me?

VICTORINE: It might seem that way, but he's actually addressing every word to his brother.

GUSTAVE: Foiled again! More wine, Hugo? Now you mustn't let me down. A river-god has got a job to do. Come on, mystify! (*Pause*) Mystify! Me!

HUGO: Er, abracadabra. It is not raining.

GUSTAVE: Brilliant! It's not!

HUGO: You are sober.

GUSTAVE: Completely true! The river-god works! Wind him up and he works.

VICTORINE: You understand our problem with Gustave now, Hugo. He is harmless enough. He gives his love as easily as he pays for his drinks.

GUSTAVE: The gutter interests me most. I have asked Édouard to paint me lying in the gutter covered in rubbish, like this. . . . (*Lies down.*) From here your boils look like mountains. Berthe will squeeze them for you. She has long nails and the icy spirit of a surgeon.

BERTHE: He should be in an asylum. We will get round to it.

HUGO: Wine. It is very good wine. I could get that way myself

with very little encouragement.
VICTORINE: Édouard is sketching you I think. No, don't keep still. It is over in a flash. There. I think he's finished. Painless wasn't it?
HUGO: I must look terrible. Excuse these pants, but I had nothing else to wear. My decision to take a swim was rather spontaneous.
BERTHE: Ah, a man of impulse. They are decent, big-hearted garments. Victorine and I are students of such drawers, aren't we, love? We have a collection which we are going to donate to the National Museum when we die. It includes the Emperor's truss. . . .
VICTORINE: The Emperor's liberty bodice.
BERTHE: His whalebone corsets—with diamonds.
VICTORINE: And his monocle, which he wears in his arse so he can watch the door for Republican spies.
GUSTAVE: Girls, you might be less vulgar with Hugo until you find out whether he's a priest or not. In his present state you can't tell whether he's religious or secular.
BERTHE: Are you a priest? Please say no.
HUGO: No, I am a sort of evangelical atheist.
VICTORINE: That will do. You're a good sport.
BERTHE: Are you married?
HUGO: Yes.
BERTHE: Do you love your wife?
HUGO: Yes.
VICTORINE: You don't! Look me in the eye and say that.
BERTHE: Are you sure? Victorine is hot for you.
HUGO: Absolutely certain.
VICTORINE: You never fancy a change?
FERDINAND: Don't answer them. They're playing with you.
BERTHE: Don't anticipate Ferdy, don't anticipate.
VICTORINE: Does your wife send you out in pants like that?
HUGO: I just grabbed a few things and put them in my case. . . .
VICTORINE: You took them off the corpse of your wife's lover.
BERTHE: There's a twinkle in your eye. You don't love your wife.
HUGO: If you could meet my wife I know you would like her.
VICTORINE: That's nothing to do with it. What I'm saying is I

bet she's worn you out. Admit it. Wives wear men out.

BERTHE: You can admit it to us. We understand.

VICTORINE: Give me ten minutes and I will make you forget your wife. It will be an experience from which you will never recover. Your whole life will change. Berthe, underneath all that I think he's blushing.

FERDINAND: Perhaps we should settle down now and let Édouard get on with his work. . . .

HUGO: Yes, here is your towel, thank you. You have been kindness itself. I hope I will find an opportunity one day to pay you back.

GUSTAVE: No! Don't go. . . .

FERDINAND: Sir, it would help. . . .

GUSTAVE: We want him to stay. He's doing no harm. Édouard doesn't mind.

FERDINAND: You are imposing on his good-nature. . . .

GUSTAVE: Édouard's got all the time in the world.

FERDINAND: My friend here doesn't want this picture completed. He has his own weird reasons which would take too long to explain. Without wishing to appear impolite, these reasons are nothing to do with wanting you here. . . .

VICTORINE: Ferdy, what a slave-driver. Édouard isn't objecting. Let him stay for a while.

GUSTAVE: Why don't I want the picture completed, Ferdy? Enlighten me?

(*Pause.* HUGO *listens, interested.*)

FERDINAND: Because you know it will get Édouard into the *Salon*.

(HUGO *moves towards the river.*)

GUSTAVE: (*Abstractedly*) Er . . . don't go, river-god, I need you. Can't you see why? You hear what this monster is saying?

FERDINAND: You are obstructing this painting, Gustave. You're frightened of it. . . .

(GUSTAVE *lunges after* HUGO *and grabs him by the foot.*)

GUSTAVE: No, don't go. Help me.

HUGO: I must get back. . . .

GUSTAVE: Édouard, do this poor fish a favour, immortalize him. Why shouldn't we share. . . .

HUGO: (*Laughing*) Why don't you want this picture finished?

GUSTAVE: I might like it! That would ruin me!
(*Pause.* HUGO *prises* GUSTAVE's *fingers off his ankle.*)
HUGO: I could stay a while. (*Smiles*) If the artist doesn't mind. Do you?
GUSTAVE: You're my only hope, river-god. If I could persuade you to transfer to being a canal-god it would be better, but I'll take you as you are, which is more than Édouard could. He would distort you, deliberately. (*Grabs* HUGO's *foot again, kisses it.*)
HUGO: (*Good-naturedly*) Come on, you can let go now. (*Struggles free.*)
GUSTAVE: My brother is mad. It has been creeping up on him for years. He will paint something, come back the next day, look at it and say—there! That is the truth. But it's in his head, not mine. It looks a mess to me. It looks unreal to me. But, Ferdy, even the girls when they're pleased with him, they say . . . yes, you've got it. That mess is the truth. . . .
FERDINAND: You're blind, Gustave. . . .
GUSTAVE: No I'm not, I'm scared. You know why? Because I'm starting to be convinced. I look at what he's painting, then at the thing itself—which is completely different—and I swell the chorus! Yes, I mouth, that's real, that's the truth. And I know it's not! So what is happening to me . . .?
(*Whistle, shouts off.* HUGO *freezes.*)
. . . I'm being bullied by him . . . this picture's the last straw. . . .
HUGO: Hush! Please. . . .
BERTHE: What's the matter?
HUGO: Just a moment. . . .
BERTHE: What is it? Are you in trouble? Is the filth after you?
GUSTAVE: A wanted man? You lucky fellow.
HUGO: I will explain later. If we could keep quiet for a moment.
(*Pause*)
FERDINAND: You will understand if I ask for that explanation.
HUGO: Let me make sure. (*Pause*) I think they've moved on. Yes, of course. It is quite simple really. I am in France illegally.
FERDINAND: You have not committed a crime?
HUGO: No.

VICTORINE: Why didn't you come in the proper way?
HUGO: They would not let me in.
VICTORINE: Why?
HUGO: They think I'm a nuisance.
VICTORINE: Why?
HUGO: Why don't you ask them?
VICTORINE: We don't talk to the filth. What have you done?
BERTHE: That's his business. . . .
VICTORINE: Do you kill tarts?
HUGO: How good is your memory?
VICTORINE: Not bad.
HUGO: There was some trouble in Paris fourteen years ago. I was involved. In all fairness I should add that France is not the only country where I am not welcome. Belgium threw me out, Prussia heaved me over the border . . . only England will have me.
VICTORINE: Why will the English have you?
HUGO: Because they do not take me seriously.
FERDINAND: I thought the English took everything seriously.
(*Pause*)
BERTHE: Hugo, there's no need to be afraid. . . .
FERDINAND: I'll have to sort this out with Édouard.
BERTHE: What's it got to do with him?
FERDINAND: This is Manet land! If the police find him here, with us, there could be a lot of trouble. It could affect Édouard's chances with the Hanging Committee for the *Salon*.
(*Pause*. GUSTAVE *hides his head, laughing*.)
BERTHE: Manet land? Does that make it holy? Ferdy, stop making such a fool of yourself. The *Salon* is a room—just that, a room. Édouard can survive without it. Stop being such a shit. You're shaming him.
FERDINAND: Édouard! He must go. We can't have trouble with the police.
VICTORINE: Ferdy, you're a disgrace. How do you think Hugo looks at us now, eh? Manet land. What a thing to say to anyone.
BERTHE: (*Walking off into the trees*) Don't you talk to me again, Ferdy. I don't want to even look at you, you collaborator!

FERDINAND: As you like. (*Coming down-stage.*) Édouard, this is a serious matter. . . .

HUGO: In a moment I will go the way I came. Monsieur Manet, I am sorry for the upset I have caused.

VICTORINE: Édouard is not asking you to go.

HUGO: I think the police have moved away.

FERDINAND: Édouard, the Emperor has complete control over the Hanging Committee. One whiff of scandal and you'll never have another painting accepted. . . .

VICTORINE: For Christ's sake, Ferdy, don't make him worse than he is!

FERDINAND: You want him to end up like the others? Living out in the provinces on butchers' portraits, no medals, no one writing about him, no one taking notice. . . . (*Returns*) That's what can happen if you're not careful.

VICTORINE: Ferdy, Édouard can take care of himself. (*Pause*) He's kept Suzanne quiet for long enough, and Léon.

FERDINAND: That doesn't involve the police. (*Turns to* HUGO.) Sir, I mean no personal offence, but I believe that man down there to be a great painter. I think he has some genius now, and will have more later. But he must have the time, the freedom, the right conditions. He is not the kind of artist who thrives on adversity.

VICTORINE: Stop poncing for him, Ferdy.

FERDINAND: No one has ever seen simple things the way he does. He will be recognized. People will come round to him. Now they are hostile, that is to be expected, but give them a few years and they will flock to him. He will be adored as he deserves to be.

HUGO: I respect your dedication. Does he?

FERDINAND: He does, but even if he didn't I would think the same.

(*Pause*)

HUGO: Sacrifices have to be made. I will go back the way I came. If the police catch me I will only be deported, not guillotined.

BERTHE: And you'd let him go, wouldn't you, Ferdy? The rest of us say no, Hugo, Édouard himself says no. We would never be so impolite as to help the filth.

HUGO: No, it is not important. I don't want to spoil your day.... (HUGO *walks towards the river.* GUSTAVE *bars his way, arms out-stretched.*)

GUSTAVE: I will not allow a river-god to go to his doom because of my brother. Édouard, that Manet mole-hill on Manet land is only a conventional, hypocritical pygmy who paints rebelliously for prizes.

FERDINAND: If there is a scandal, Gustave, your mother will hear of this! You're being stupid and irresponsible.

GUSTAVE: Ferdy, if you were a better sculptor you wouldn't be so concerned that Édouard should be a better painter.

BERTHE: And we never help the filth, Ferdy! Never! Let me ever catch you lifting a finger for them and I'll get someone to make mincemeat out of you. I mean it!

VICTORINE: Don't kid yourself about the filth, Hugo. They're bad.

BERTHE: Things have changed. These are the Emperor's police now.

VICTORINE: Once they get hold of you ... finish.

HUGO: I don't think they'll go that far. I'm not a French citizen.

BERTHE: They'll just make you disappear. Ask the anarchists. They drop out of sight like peas off your plate.

HUGO: Really, I think it would be better if I went....

BERTHE: No you're not. You stay where you are. You can't be sure the filth have moved on. Have something to eat and a few drinks. Give them time to get miles away.

HUGO: They could come back.

VICTORINE: Then we'll let them have Gustave. He has been doing back-street abortions....

GUSTAVE: Purely for practice.

BERTHE: And Ferdy, well, he's got a record. He is the worst sculptor to come out of Zalt-Bommel. It would be a wise move to take away his mallet and lock him up for life.

HUGO: I must admit, that water looks colder every minute.

BERTHE: He's going to stay.

VICTORINE: Come on, Édouard, come and drink with us. We're not doing any more work today. Take a rest, relax. Leave it.

(*Pause*) Miserable louse. (*Angrily*) Oh, give up on it, will you. Who wants to look at us mixed up like that? Come and get drunk . . . oh, suit yourself then. . . .

BERTHE: I'll be very straight with you, Hugo. You're my kind of man. I know there's a real chin under all that hair. (*Pause*) I fancy you.

GUSTAVE: When Berthe says that, most men either run up the white flag or run up the street. What are you going to do?

HUGO: Remind her that I am old enough to be her father.

BERTHE: You think that worries me? Hugo, I have to take men who collapse when they take off their corsets, men who have to pull themselves up with a chair . . . so you? You're perfect. (*Pause*) All my men have boils.

(BERTHE *swiftly kisses* HUGO's *leg*. FERDINAND *leans back, adjusts his hat.*)

FERDINAND: (*Casually*) What is it like in England now?

HUGO: They have the fastest machines you have ever seen, and the worst poverty. It is an extreme country.

FERDINAND: Extreme? The English? Aren't they slow?

HUGO: Watch England. It is becoming very strong. May I beg another glass of this wine? It is doing me a world of good.

VICTORINE: I have never been to England.

HUGO: Go if you can. It is very interesting.

VICTORINE: Are people rich?

HUGO: Moving ahead, very quickly.

VICTORINE: Are you rich?

HUGO: No.

VICTORINE: Why do you live there?

HUGO: Who else will have me?

VICTORINE: Why do they keep chucking you out?

HUGO: You know what's the worst? I am Prussian! Yet I'm thrown out of Prussia! What do you think of that?

GUSTAVE: I think that is very strange.

(FERDINAND *walks down-stage and sits on the edge of the apron, sipping a glass of wine.*)

River-god, you haven't answered Victorine's question.

HUGO: Give me time. I'm thinking about it.

FERDINAND: Édouard, Léon. I'm afraid Suzanne is too reticent.

Much as I'd like to leave you free to concentrate on your work, as the boy's uncle I must try and protect his interests. I know the problem is the *Salon*. If you admit paternity there may be a scandal and the Committee will shut you out. So any public recognition of Léon is out, but I think you should tell the boy you are his father in private. He would appreciate that. I think he suspects the truth, but he doesn't *know*, which puts him in a difficult position. Édouard, he only wants to be real. Let him exist, let him live in the full knowledge that he is a genuine Manet. Give him the proof he needs. A signature on a piece of paper which we will lodge with a lawyer. You are my son. I will get him to agree not to publicize his authenticity until you are dead. How about that as an idea? (*Pause*) You are unmoved. Then I must ask you to bring to mind another boy, Alexandre, your little apprentice and brush-washer from the old studio. He looked on you as his father. He loved you, but you kept him at arm's length, didn't you? You kept the poor child an orphan in spirit as well as fact. You wouldn't join in his make-believe, which was cruel. Do you remember the day you found him hanging in the studio? Yes, next to your other pictures. Do you want Léon to go the same way and kill himself because you will not admit to his creation? (*Pause*) All right, forget it. I didn't hope for much when I brought it up. Carry on with your work and we'll sort something out. . . . But I feel it, Édouard, I feel it! You know, I never accepted the post-mortem verdict on Alexandre, did you? The boy's brain can't have been infected . . . no, no, not at that age, surely? You've got to be sexually mature before you can contract it, and he wasn't, was he?

HUGO: I think they threw me out because I am not a Prussian, I am an internationalist, a citizen of the world.

VICTORINE: Does it say that on your passport?

HUGO: No. Nor does it say under 'Profession' man of ideas. But that's what I am. You see these boils, blast them?! They are the physical consequences of finding ideas. I have to spend ten, twelve hours a day, reading. The benches are hard, my diet is not what it should be, my clothing, is rough, my skin sensitive . . . so, boils. One bursts, another heals, another starts. See the scars all over my legs, and my backside too. . . .

GUSTAVE: We'll take your word for it.

VICTORINE: Tell us some of your ideas, or will it give you mouth ulcers?

HUGO: My doctor recommends swimming. It is a circulation problem. (*Pause*) First, that Man has an economic destiny. Secondly, that though it is inevitable, being destined, it can be accelerated. Thirdly, it is governed by science.

GUSTAVE: Would your idea enable me to qualify earlier and obtain a profitable practice in a fashionable quarter of Paris?

HUGO: It would not, I'm afraid.

GUSTAVE: Then, as an instrument of change, you are as much use to me as my brother's masterpieces. You both just lie there and expect us to stagger back, blinded with amazement.

HUGO: That kind of reaction does help on the days when one is feeling insecure.

GUSTAVE: I think you are some kind of confused god like my brother. Do you keep yourself?

BERTHE: Gustave, why in hell do you always have to know that?

GUSTAVE: It matters. I love this man. I pledged myself to him. I have a right to know whether he is a parasite or not. Who keeps you?

HUGO: My friends, my mother, my colleagues.

GUSTAVE: You have no paid employment?

HUGO: No.

GUSTAVE: Brother! (*Hugs him.*) You are one of us.

HUGO: I have employment though. I am in the middle of writing a very long book. No, don't look hopeful. It is not a novel. My guess is that it would bore you to death. It does me, sometimes.

GUSTAVE: I knew you were my brother in spirit. You are as useless as I am. A book no one will want to read? How will you sell it, by weight?

HUGO: Or propping up furniture. But not government furniture.

GUSTAVE: Ah!

HUGO: You are excited.

GUSTAVE: Édouard, paint this man's picture quickly and we can sell it to the police.

VICTORINE: Is that all you do? Scribble?

HUGO: Yes, nearly.

VICTORINE: You don't have to come to Paris in secret to scribble.

HUGO: No. I have come to meet some people. They invited me over.

VICTORINE: What's this book about?

HUGO: Economics.

VICTORINE: I don't know what that is.

HUGO: It's the science of money. I am a scientific writer.

VICTORINE: You come to Paris just to see some friends? You take a risk like that?

HUGO: They have asked me for some help.

VICTORINE: About money?

HUGO: Yes, in a way.

VICTORINE: Then you can give Berthe and me a hand while you're here. We're broke.

HUGO: (*Laughing*) I have to work on a big scale.

VICTORINE: We can get you as many people as you can handle. If you are good with money why haven't you got any?

HUGO: I didn't say I was interested in making it, just studying it.

VICTORINE: Oh. Just looking at it? (*Pause*) I think you must be crazy.

HUGO: There are others who agree with you.

VICTORINE: But I'll read your book. I wouldn't miss that.

FERDINAND: Hugo, I'm quite interested . . . er, casually you know. Is this some pet theory you've got? I think I've read everything there is to read on economics, and there's not much except for Smith and Ricardo. . . .

GUSTAVE: Smith and Ricardo, an amazing double-act will jump through a hoop of fire wearing leg-irons, hair shirts and Spanish sombreros. Hugo, Ferdy has read the titles, the titles. He is trying to impress you.

FERDINAND: Will you shut up, Gustave? Stop making such a virtue out of your ignorance.

GUSTAVE: Smith and Ricardo. Pah!

FERDINAND: Go and do something elsewhere. Go on, I'm tired of you.
GUSTAVE: I don't do what you tell me to do.
FERDINAND: You're a stupid drunken baby, Gustave. Go on, leave us in peace for a while.
HUGO: There is no need. . . .
FERDINAND: There are times when one must insist with Gustave. He is spoilt. We listen most of the time, we endure him for Édouard's sake. Go on Gustave, do some fishing.
GUSTAVE: I don't want to.
FERDINAND: Do some fishing or I'll sort you out!
GUSTAVE: All right.
(GUSTAVE *goes to the boat, takes out a rod and reel and starts to thread the line, attach the hook and float. Pause.*)
FERDINAND: That's better. Yes, Hugo, money. Obviously it's interesting.
HUGO: I don't limit myself to money. My theme is bigger.
FERDINAND: But the main problems have been solved I think, you'll admit that. There is a steady improvement all round.
HUGO: Yes. The present system is creating wealth at a phenomenal rate, unprecedented in human economic history. There has never been such prosperity. Productivity is rising, communications improving, trade booming.
FERDINAND: So what are you saying that's so dangerous? That it will suddenly stop? Collapse?
HUGO: Oh no, it will go on like this. There may be temporary depressions, bad harvests, but in general the economy of Europe will carry on growing. I think we have thirty, forty years of it to look forward to. Yes, it will be a period of unprecedented development.
FERDINAND: Well, that's a relief.
GUSTAVE: Victorine, come and help me catch a fish.
VICTORINE: (*Getting up*) Poor Gustave. Are you miserable? (*Strokes his head.*) It sounds as though the Suez Canal might work after all.
GUSTAVE: I wish I could sing an aria from Smith and Ricardo.
VICTORINE: Ferdy will get tough with you again.
FERDINAND: So, if you were an investor, Hugo, you'd recommend

a working knowledge of economics?

HUGO: It is the science of the future.

GUSTAVE: Tran-ta-ra-ra! The briefest of overtures introduces Smith and Ricardo's latest musical masterpiece, a new opera entitled, 'Doom In The Diggings' or 'Holes In Very Fine Sand Are Impossible'. A hush, the hush of paper money sleeping on gold. The curtain rises on the forecourt of the Temple of Plenty. Pause. Enter Industry in a cast-iron helmet, bare-breasted and bathed in the light of Dawn, sharp eyes searching a silent horizon for smoke. Good morning! she trills to the welcoming hordes of Suez Canal labourers up to their ears in night-shift sand. Good morning! they roar in the key of B Minor. How goes it? she asks in a commanding contralto only rivalled by the assembled fog-horns of the British navy as a thousand ships sail into view, hurrying to be first through the new international waterway. Where are you all headed for, you mercantile matelots? thunders the bass-baritone from Boulogne who is playing Capital tonight. A golden future, sing the men of the merchant marine augmented by ten tenors from Trieste, two from Tannenberg and one from Toronto in favour of transatlantic trade. We are all going to make a f-o-r-t-u-n-e! How? boom a billion basses from Birmingham, Bali and New Brunswick. Ferrying flax, fodder, fol-de-rols and farinaceous foods to Hong Kong, Korea and Christmas Island, sings a solo soprano salivating sideways over her superlative salary. Exploiter! exhales an arsehole from Amsterdam! Materialist! moos an adroit but atrocious alto from Avignon 'aving acute agony with 'is 'igh A's and aitches. 'Oo cares? calls a counter-tenor to his crumbling coloratura who has tits trapped in the oddly included accordion in the almighty orchestra. No one! crescendoes a chorus of churls in chains on their way to China 'oping to re-open the Opium trade. Ya got the money? Ya got the ending? Ya got the score? A final aria by a boy treble bleeding from the nose, entitled Man is monkey (Do ah win, do ah lose?) then take out the K and make it money, monkey without the K, without the kudos, without the Christ, without the credence, and the curtain comes tumbling down! Rapturous applause! Smith and Ricardo are called to the stage! Author! Author! We have a hit on our hands tonight! The Suez Canal is filled with champagne and the crocodiles weep with alcoholic remorse, of course!

FERDINAND: Édouard, I can't stand this fool any more. I'm going home.

BERTHE: Ferdy, don't be such a wet blanket.

FERDINAND: He is deliberately wasting our time.

GUSTAVE: Ferdy, I'll be quiet. I promise. (*Takes a jar out of the boat.*) You carry on with your apology for economics, Hugo. (*Pause*) Well, go on. Ignore me. (*Opens the jar.*)

HUGO: Many of the basic principles of economics. . . .

GUSTAVE: (*Taking out a live worm*) Dug them in the garden this morning. The manure-pile is teeming with them, millions of red worms.

HUGO: (*Laughing*) I surrender.

GUSTAVE: This is a Manet worm. See, Ferdy? He's wriggling. (*Holds it up.*) Édouard, part of the family portrait! Keep still you brute! Now, the hook. . . .

VICTORINE: Well, don't show us! We don't want to see.

GUSTAVE: The worm is about to start his working life. Hugo is delighted aren't you? This Manet worm was useless until this moment, now it is about to become economically viable. It can't feel anything. It's quite stupid . . . but useful. Right? I'm going to put it on the hook. . . .

(VICTORINE *slaps his hand and the worm drops to the ground.* GUSTAVE *goes to stamp on it but* HUGO *covers the worm with his foot, then picks it up.*)

HUGO: No. Give me the jar.

(GUSTAVE *gives the jar to* HUGO. *He puts the worm back, holds out his hand for the top.* GUSTAVE *hands it over.* HUGO *carefully puts it on, holds the jar up to look at the worms, then replaces the jar in the boat.*)

GUSTAVE: Then I'll have to use bread.

FERDINAND: (*Shrugging*) I give up, Édouard, I give up.

(GUSTAVE *takes a piece of bread, goes to the boat, sits on the gunwhale, baits his hook with bread-flake, then casts into the*

(*river, settles the line, then sits very still. Pause. He turns, smiles at* HUGO, *winks, turns back. Pause.* BERTHE *pats* FERDINAND's *hand, gets up, smiles at* HUGO, *then walks down-stage.*)

BERTHE: Édouard, could you ask for a better life? (*Pause*) Of us all you have got closest to doing what you want to do with your time. These are little arguments, pinpricks. Gustave does love you. When his brother is accepted and praised, you watch him then. What he wants more than anything is to see people *buying* your work. Then it will be all right. You will be completely vindicated. It is this in-between time, while you are building up your reputation, that is difficult for him. When you make the break-through, Gustave will be on top of the world. And, you know what else will happen? Ferdy will get less interested, because this is the kind of moment he enjoys—watching something grow. Remember I said that. We'll see if I'm right. . . .

GUSTAVE: Ah!

HUGO: A bite?

GUSTAVE: A knock, a nibble. Here we go again.

HUGO: Strike then.

GUSTAVE: Which is exactly what you said to the Egyptians, you radical swine!

(HUGO *laughs.*)

BERTHE: The good thing about it is the way you keep us all together. We fight, who doesn't, but each day there is someone suggesting that we go here for dinner, go there for a walk. For me, I enjoy it when you join in and talk and tell us why you see people like you do, and why you choose one light in preference to another . . . the technicalities, the ideas, I know that you can't always explain down to the bottom level, but that's where this bond comes in. There is a bond. We all feel it, we've all got it. There have been times when I wished more than anything that I could be released from its responsibilities, cleaned and cured. I know Victorine gets the same way. But we always come back for more. You know why?

HUGO: The Suez Canal, my friend, is being dug by slaves.

GUSTAVE: Slaves, by definition, cannot stop work. If they do, they die.
HUGO: The Egyptian labourer is in the same position. Yet he chooses to starve. Why? (*Pause*) When Rameses the Second started the original canal two thousand years ago, it was dug by slaves, the same slaves that built the Pyramids. This canal, two thousand years later, is being dug by slaves as well, and if they finish it in their present conditions of employment they will have raised an equal monument to the pharaohs of contemporary capitalism.
GUSTAVE: You mean there's been another canal?
HUGO: It was a failure also.
GUSTAVE: We're repeating a failure? I've invested my dead father's money in an ancient flop? Things are worse than I thought. The dead are investing in the dying.
BERTHE: We're moths round a flame. (*Turns to* HUGO.) Give Édouard ten francs and he'll paint your boils out for you. He could even improve the size of your brain.
(*Pause*. HUGO *looks into the audience and laughs*.)
HUGO: That is the kind of help I need.
GUSTAVE: (*Twitching the rod*) There's something moving down there. (*Pause*) At last we know what the Sphinx is smiling at. Me, the small-time French investor, the small-time French revolutionary, the small-time French lover, the small-time French father, French letter, pox and leave.
VICTORINE: Will you tell us about your wife, please, Hugo.
HUGO: My wife?
VICTORINE: Tell us about her. Is she good-looking?
HUGO: My wife is a beautiful woman.
BERTHE: Are you sure?
HUGO: Of course I'm sure. She was the most beautiful girl in the town I lived in ... by far. There was no one to match her.
BERTHE: *Was?*
HUGO: She could have had any husband she liked.
VICTORINE: How long have you been together?
HUGO: Twenty years.
VICTORINE: Hell.

BERTHE: No wonder he's in love with science. Twenty years? Twenty minutes is long enough for me. Where is she from?
HUGO: My home town, it's on the French border. . . .
BERTHE: Don't be smart, Hugo. I mean what *class* is she from? The town doesn't matter.
(*Pause*)
HUGO: She is from an aristocratic family.
BERTHE: I could tell.
HUGO: How?
BERTHE: The way you said *beautiful*.
HUGO: Her brother is the Prussian Minister of the Interior, her father was a Privy Councillor. How did I say that?
BERTHE: You might just as well have stuck your finger up my nose.
VICTORINE: Another one. (*Sighs*) Paris is full of them. If they're not Prussians they're Russians, if they're not Russians they're Rumanians. Hugo, you're a deadhead with a beautiful aristo wife. We've known hundreds. You outnumber the poor.
HUGO: Exiles don't ask to be exiles.
BERTHE: And you've never been unfaithful to this aristo?
HUGO: I've not been unfaithful.
VICTORINE: I thought there was only one way to say that.
FERDINAND: Girls, this is very discourteous.
BERTHE: Get out. He can't get away with that. Come on, Hugo, you're telling lies.
FERDINAND: Don't answer. They're hopelessly nosey.
HUGO: I think perhaps I should.
BERTHE: See Ferdy? He makes up his own mind. Go on, tell us about how you've been faithful.
HUGO: When we left Prussia—let's say we were invited to leave for a while—we came here, to Paris. One of my wife's servants followed us here—a girl.
VICTORINE: Aha!
HUGO: She has been with us all the time. Then, after twenty years, she needs me. My servant comes to me and says she needs me. Up until that moment there was nothing.
(*Pause*)
BERTHE: You agreed?

HUGO: It was not a negotiation. She made it plain, I must have you with me. So I went. She even bought a new bed.

VICTORINE: You left your wife?

HUGO: No.

VICTORINE: You deceived your wife under her own roof?

HUGO: My wife knew. If anyone *agreed*, it was her.

BERTHE: That is magnificent! Hooray for such a wife. Bring her over here!

VICTORINE: And is your servant happy now?

HUGO: A child was born. I think that was what she really wanted.

BERTHE: Your child?

HUGO: *A* child.

BERTHE: Do you have children by the aristo?

HUGO: Yes, three daughters.

VICTORINE: How old are they?

HUGO: A little younger than you, but not too much.

VICTORINE: Are they good-looking?

HUGO: To me . . . yes, I think they are anyway.

VICTORINE: But you'd never let them be tarts, would you?

HUGO: With the world as it is all of us are tarts, aren't we?

BERTHE: Well said, if you mean it. If you don't, shit on you.

VICTORINE: I think he means it. He's sentimental. Give me a few minutes and I could make him cry.

BERTHE: Hugo, if you stayed long enough I think we might need you. Be warned. You must have more than enough women in your life.

HUGO: They're all over the place. Every door I go through has a woman on the other side.

VICTORINE: Take us home with you. We'll polish your boots and buy the beds.

HUGO: There's no room. (*Gets up with the towel round his shoulders and a glass of wine in his hand.*) Monsieur Manet, you have good friends. (*Walks down-stage.*) That is a kind of genius in iself. (*Lowers his voice.*) May I ask, in confidence, if I am completely unknown to you? I was under the impression that Paris was one of my lucky towns . . . somewhere that actually remembered. Oh, it was a long time ago, years. You were a child no doubt, interested in other things. But if you are seeing things differently, and you feel that certainty—is there a more wonderful sensation?—of being close to the true reality—I might have been instrumental in bringing that gift to you. We may be looking through the same pair of glasses, you through one lens, me the other. I am not asking you to admit anything at this stage. It is only a chance. Your pictures may be laughable. But if they sing aloud with change, if they ring out like bells over this city—well, you might try and bring my name to mind from all your schoolbooks and bibles. Not an arresting title, no. Think of your own process. You take the light, you make it manifest within the eye, you give it sense and proportion—perhaps. That is my style, too. We should talk. . . .

GUSTAVE: (*Throwing the rod down*) Close the Seine! All the French fish are migrating to Mexico! And you, river-god, you are the underwater, under-cover agitator who provoked the Egyptian fellaheen and made them throw down their shovels! I see now, you are a dangerous myth indeed! Stand up and fight!

HUGO: I deny all charges. I am innocent your worship.

FERDINAND: (*Coming up behind him*) Did you recognize your child?

HUGO: I beg your pardon.

FERDINAND: The servant's child. Do you accept the servant's child?

HUGO: Well, the position. . . .

FERDINAND: (*Furiously*) DO YOU ACCEPT THE SERVANT'S CHILD?

HUGO: What do you mean? He lives in our house.

FERDINAND: *Your* house, Prussian. You own it. Now, the child: does it have your name?

HUGO: What is my name?

FERDINAND: So, you don't own it. You have not given it your name. It is not called Moor.

HUGO: It is not called Moor.

FERDINAND: And you are not ashamed?

HUGO: The boy is the equal of the others. . . .

FERDINAND: But you have not given him your name. You will not publicly admit that his blood is yours.

HUGO: His blood is his own. I do not contribute to that view of society. I reject inheritance.
(*Pause*)

FERDINAND: Convenient.

HUGO: (*Angrily*) I have already lost four children! Did I own those?

FERDINAND: Losing presupposes owning.

HUGO: When he grows up he can take any name he likes. (*Pause*) It is philosophy that needs my name, not children.

FERDINAND: If you say so. I don't know your thoughts.

HUGO: I can even forgive Christianity much because it taught us to worship the child, but I must remain absolutely conscious that my scientific discovery marks a development in the history of the human race, not one individual, no matter how precious. (*Pause*) I can have a thousand children and still leave nothing of myself behind.

FERDINAND: I understand.

HUGO: Do you?

FERDINAND: Please accept my apologies. I did not mean to raise my voice to you.

HUGO: That was the agreement. She has the child. It was all she wanted from me. . . .

FERDINAND: Yes.

HUGO: Do you think that there are not enough names that people can call me without my providing more? They attack my ideas, why should I give them the chance to attack *me*? She knows that, the mother knows that, she would never want to expose me to public censure. . . .

FERDINAND: Of course.
(*From off-stage right a shout, 'Hello!'*)

VICTORINE: Quiet! What was that?
(*Off, 'Hello!'*)

BERTHE: It's the filth!

VICTORINE: Hugo, they sound very close. . . .
(*Off, 'Hello!'*)

GUSTAVE: They're on the island!

FERDINAND: That's it, we've had it. They're going to find him here.

VICTORINE: Hugo, put my dress on, and the bonnet.

FERDINAND: Édouard, I appeal to you . . . sort this out.

(HUGO *drags the dress over his head.* VICTORINE *and* BERTHE *help him, putting the bonnet on his head.* VICTORINE *then drops her cloak and sits down, naked.*)

VICTORINE: Go and squat in the trees.

HUGO: Squat?

VICTORINE: Look like you're having a piss.

(HUGO *goes into the trees and stands there.*)

Not like a man, you twat! Like a woman. Squat!

(HUGO *squats.* BERTHE *drops the top of her shift and exposes a breast.* GUSTAVE *and* FERDINAND *freeze as* ÉRIQUE *enters. He is a thin, sharp man wearing white trousers and a vest.*)

ÉRIQUE: Excuse me. I'm looking for a friend.

VICTORINE: Will I do?

ÉRIQUE: I'm sorry to disturb you but it is quite important.

(BERTHE *snatches up a knife from the picnic and holds it against* ÉRIQUE's *back ribs.*)

BERTHE: What do you want? Don't turn round or I'll spear your kidneys. Papers.

ÉRIQUE: Back pocket.

GUSTAVE: Who is this friend you're looking for?

(BERTHE *carefully removes some folded papers from* ÉRIQUE's *back pocket and hands them to* FERDINAND.)

ÉRIQUE: That is my business.

VICTORINE: If you are the filth you had better start composing a farewell speech.

FERDINAND: What am I supposed to do with these?

BERTHE: Look at them. Who is he?

(FERDINAND *opens the papers and scrutinizes them.*)

ÉRIQUE: (*Nodding at* HUGO *who is still squatting, his back to him*) Who is that?

VICTORINE: My mother.

ÉRIQUE: What is she doing?

VICTORINE: She's having a piss.

(*Pause*)

ÉRIQUE: She must have a bladder like a horse.
FERDINAND: His name is Érique Claraud . . . he's a pattern-maker.
HUGO: Érique, it is you . . . (*Turns*)
ÉRIQUE: Karl, thank God we've found you. . . .
HUGO: Sssh! (*Comes across to* ÉRIQUE.) I told you not to follow me.
ÉRIQUE: We were worried that you'd drowned. There's a boat at the top end of the island. . . .
VICTORINE: (*Putting the cloak back on*) You know each other . . . all right. That is fine.
BERTHE: (*Dropping the knife*) He looks good doesn't he? Disguise is obviously your strong point, Karl. (*Puts her breast back.*)
HUGO: I came in illegally. You don't expect me to use my own name do you?
BERTHE: To us, yes. So who are you?
ÉRIQUE: He is the guest of my organization.
VICTORINE: And what is that?
ÉRIQUE: We have a friendly society.
VICTORINE: You think you're the only one?
ÉRIQUE: It's a working-men's organization.
VICTORINE: So is ours, only the hours are longer.
FERDINAND: He works in the cannon-foundry at Billancourt Arsenal.

(*Pause.* FERDINAND *gives the papers back to* ÉRIQUE. *Pause. They look at* HUGO. *He starts to take* VICTORINE's *dress off. It is a struggle. No one helps him. They stare at him in silence.*)

VICTORINE: Careful! You're stretching it. . . .
ÉRIQUE: Then give him a hand.
VICTORINE: No. (*Pause*) It doesn't matter. I'll have to burn it now anyway.

(HUGO *holds out the dress to* VICTORINE. *She indicates that he should throw it on the ground where it was originally. He obliges, tossing the bonnet after it.*)

HUGO: Don't waste a good dress. Érique, have you got a few francs?

(ÉRIQUE *gives* HUGO *some money out of his pocket.*)

HUGO: Here, get it cleaned, and the towel. (*Offers the money.*)

VICTORINE: No.
>(HUGO *keeps his hand out, then shrugs, gives the money back to* ÉRIQUE.)

FERDINAND: Will you go now?

HUGO: Have you any idea of the conditions these men work under?

FERDINAND: I am not asking for explanations.

HUGO: Half the artillery for the French army and navy is made at Billancourt. . . .

FERDINAND: We're not involved and we don't want to be.

VICTORINE: What are you, an arms-dealer?

ÉRIQUE: No, he's not. You can cut that out. . . .

VICTORINE: How do we know? What do you want from a cannon-foundry? Justice?

(*Pause*)

HUGO: Where are the police now?

ÉRIQUE: They're a long way off now. There's nothing to worry about. We've got your clothes in the boat.

GUSTAVE: Burn them. Let him sail back to England like that.

ÉRIQUE: Now stop this. He is my friend, so watch out. . . .

GUSTAVE: Get off our land! My land!

HUGO: Why have you turned against me? What is all the excitement about?

FERDINAND: A scientist with a gun? An economist with a cannon?

HUGO: You cannot just argue on paper. . . .

FERDINAND: Not such a joke now, eh Gustave? You get rid of him. . . .

ÉRIQUE: He'll go when he's ready.

VICTORINE: Two-faced bastard!

ÉRIQUE: Shut up! You don't know what you're talking about.

(*Pause*)

VICTORINE: If there's no blood in the streets then no one is having a good time. We were kids at the last lot. Berthe had to search for her old man under a ton of straw at the morgue!

BERTHE: I'll deal with that. (*Pause*) But I can rely on you to hate Louis Napoléon, can't I?

ÉRIQUE: Hate him? Destroyed him! He has written a whole book against the Emperor! He's torn him to pieces!

BERTHE: Then I'd like the name of the sod who put him back together again.

FERDINAND: Listen, both of you, the revolution, if you can bless that brawl with such a name, was the Emperor's birthday. Without it France would still be a republic . . . after that fiasco you couldn't even talk about democracy. The revolution made the Emperor inevitable.
(Pause)

BERTHE: I'd like to ask you a question for myself.

ÉRIQUE: Karl, let's leave these bourgeois pigs to get on with it. No questions! We're going.

HUGO: What is the question?

BERTHE: Why does a servant woman want you as the father of her child and your homeland close its borders to you?
(Pause)

HUGO: I'll send you a copy of my book.

BERTHE: I don't read much, even under pressure.

HUGO: In the revolution of eighteen forty-eight in Paris, I had cause to go into a brothel. There was a sign painted on the ceiling of every room—Respect Your Comrade Sister! I like to think that my servant, and my home, give me equal credit in their own way.

VICTORINE: You, in a brothel? With a beautiful aristo wife? Well.

HUGO: I went there to deliver some newspapers.

BERTHE: You went there to sell newspapers?

HUGO: They only cost a few sous.

BERTHE: You took them newspapers, you'll send us books. What have you got against tarts?

VICTORINE: You're a stinking priest!

ÉRIQUE: Bitch, you'll get the back of my hand!

HUGO: No need, calm down . . . yes, Victorine, if I must be called a priest because I have beliefs. . . .

FERDINAND: A scientific priest with a gun. Your creed must be complicated.

HUGO: Not at all. I am a materialist. I detest poverty.

GUSTAVE: You assured me that you had no shares in the Suez Canal.
(Pause)

FERDINAND: Materialism is already triumphant! That *is* Capitalism!

HUGO: It must be adapted to the needs of the majority. As a faith it must fit the poor. There are two virulent diseases—Christianity and Capitalism.

GUSTAVE: A logical diagnosis by an impoverished Jew. (*Pause*) In those pants even a man as deceitful as you cannot keep a secret.

ÉRIQUE: Shit! I'm not having that!

(ÉRIQUE *hits* GUSTAVE, *knocking him down.* FERDINAND *grabs* ÉRIQUE's *arms.*)

HUGO: That was a stupid thing to do. Go and stand over there and keep quiet!

(FERDINAND *releases* ÉRIQUE *who walks to the left and stands by himself, his back to* GUSTAVE. HUGO *offers* GUSTAVE *his hand. He takes it.* HUGO *pulls him to his feet.*)

Are you hurt?

(GUSTAVE *shakes his head, pulls his hand away.*)

Come to England, Gustave. Come and see me. I could use you. I could train you. Yes, I could. You have a lot to offer me. I could use you like you will never use yourself. Being with you here has upset me. I cannot stand waste. When I send you back to France, you should have a chance to outstrip Édouard. (*Pause*) No? Take some time to think about it. If you do change your mind, come and visit me. My name is Doctor Marx and I live near Hampstead Heath in London. You will find me walking on Parliament Hill any day after lunch. (*Walks down-stage.*) Well, now I'll get out of your way so you can carry on with your work. I hope your view of reality is not as unpopular as mine is with the authorities. Perhaps you can get away with more in painting. We will leave from another part of the island. I don't think there is much danger of us being seen. Do you care if I am? (*Pause*) Your manners are impeccable. If they arrest me, you and I might get closer together. There are Hanging Committees and Hanging Committees. (*Pause*) And tell your brother that my offer is sincere. I can give him the chance to make something of his life.

ÉRIQUE: Karl, I think we should be getting back if you don't mind. . . .

HUGO: Goodbye, Monsieur Manet, and good luck. (*Turns, walks back.*) Goodbye to all of you, and thanks for sharing your wine with me. (*Pause*) Gustave. . . .

(GUSTAVE *does not respond, his back turned to* HUGO. HUGO *whispers over his shoulder.*)

Tombs in Rome, graves in Egypt. That's not a wise investment. Sell them out and join us.

(HUGO *exits left with* ÉRIQUE.)

FERDINAND: (*Clapping his hands*) Back to your places. There's not much light left.

(BERTHE, VICTORINE, FERDINAND *and* GUSTAVE *swiftly rearrange the scene until it is set exactly the same as the opening of the play, then slide into their original poses and positions.*)

(*Lights fade to Blackout.*)

(*The picture is Édouard Manet's 'Dejeuner sur l'Herbe' which now hangs in the Jeu de Paume, Musée de l'Impressionnisme, Paris.*)